Tannin of Ironhaven

Mike Conley

&

Kylynn Conley

Published by Mike Conley, 2023

Also published on Kindle Vella as Tannin of Ironhaven

The characters and events portrayed in this book are fictitious. Any similarity to real persons, living or dead, is coincidental and not intended by the author.

No part of this book may be reproduced, or stored in a retrieval system, or transmitted in any form or by any means, electronic, mechanical, photocopying, recording, or otherwise, without the express written permission of the publisher.

Tannin of Ironhaven

First edition. Feb 11, 2023

Copyright © 2023 Mike Conley.

Written by Mike Conley and Kylynn Conley

All rights reserved.

Other work by
Mike Conley

The After — Book 1 of the Afterverse

Destiny's Crow — Book 2 of the Afterverse (2023)

Past the Fall — serialized story on Kindle Vella (2022-2023)

Adam & Elese - An Afterverse Story — serialized story on Kindle Vella and will be on Kindle Unlimited and Amazon mid-2023

Social Links

Author site:
https://miketconley.com

Facebook Author page:
https://www.facebook.com/authormikeconley

TikTok:
https://www.tiktok.com/@miketconley_author

Instagram:
https://www.instagram.com/miketconley

YouTube Channel:
https://www.youtube.com/channel/UC3PEspi2DIy3Gfh8h-LMSQg

Author Mike Conley discord server:
https://discord.gg/22BBS3zC2B

Dedication

We dedicate this short story to Kylynn Conley, who co-authored the story and had creative control over the creation with her first dip into the authoring world. At age 11, this is a great first exposure and I hope she picks up the craft on her own someday.

We would like to thank Margaret Conley, wife and mother, for her patience and alpha reading of this book.

We would also like to take a moment and thank you for reading this. We are book lovers too and we appreciate you taking your time to read our work. Take a moment to pat yourself on the back for supporting an indie author.

Thank you!

CHAPTER ONE

SO THAT HAPPENED

I often fantasize about grander things in outlandish worlds. Imagining a life I know I should live in a fantasy world of my making. A life I certainly would be living if the universe was fair and just, but I've long left fair and just behind. I'm now living in the remains of a family my parents destroyed. Constantly shuffled between houses, but I endure. I endure, because I know in another year, I'll be gone. Gone to make a life of my own in some college in a town far enough away that I'm not expected to come back every weekend. It won't be easy, but it will be a

world of my making.

While staring at the large crack in the wall, I wish for my old bedroom. The much bigger and nicer bedroom I had before they split up and sold the house I grew up in. A bedroom with a life that seems like such a distant memory that may as well it never have existed. Now I have two rooms and each is half the size and are on opposite sides of town in very similar townhouses. No use wishing for things that cannot be, as experience proves it won't change anything. It's much better to get out of the house. After all, I have plans for this evening.

I pull myself from the bed and shuffle to the bathroom to check my hair for what must be the fifth time. I toss around my blond locks a little to give them an intentionally messy look. And now my hair looks exactly like it did before I touched it. I'm always self-conscious before a date. At 17, I think I'm pretty good looking. My girlfriend Heidi tells me I'm a solid eight, but I assume she is trying to build my ego a little.

I still have a little while before I must leave, so I grab a few crackers to settle my stomach. No need for Heidi to notice it grumbling. We have been dating for four months, but I still get nervous for the first few minutes when we hang out. After those

initial nerves calm down, we are great together. Heidi and I started dating a few weeks after my parents split up, and early on, she was a brilliant listener. Her parents divorced a few years back, and she understands what I'm going through, and it is great to talk to her about it. I don't know how I would have gotten through the initial weeks without her.

After killing a few minutes by watching whatever was on the cartoon network, I head out to warm up my car. It is twice as old as I am and needs a lot of pampering. I spend a few minutes scraping the windows, then hop in and start my short drive to Ironhaven city park. The parking lot backs up to Heidi's dad's house. I use this lot as it is quicker than the route to the front because detours from road construction that did not get finished before the snow came.

I pull into the parking spot just behind Heidi's dad's townhouse complex. Checking my cell phone, it shows I'm a few minutes early. I get out of my car so I can greet her like a gentleman as she comes over the small hill. After about 15 minutes with her not showing up, I get worried. I'm unlocking my phone to text her when it alerts me she just sent a message.

Heidi: *We have always been honest with each other and I*

want to show you the respect of keeping that going

I don't feel like things are working out romantically for us

I don't think it is either of our faults, it just doesn't seem like we are compatible and I think it is best to end things

I read the messages five times before it sinks in, then my legs about give out and I fall back into my car. It's at that moment I realize it is over. Dumped after what I thought was four great months. She just broke up using a text message. Ouch!

It's 20 minutes before I moved or even dared to think. My soul is hurting, my heart is sad, but my mind is angry. I should leave, but I don't think it's a good idea to drive on the major streets without calming down. I move my car to the far side of the parking lot near the lake so it doesn't appear that I'm still waiting for her. Then I decide it's a good idea to take a walk along the lake. They keep that walk de-iced so it should be fine, and if not, I have traction straps for my shoes in my coat pocket.

After strolling for several minutes, I notice a couple a few years older than me playing on the ice. The lake ices over nicely and people use it to ice-skate. Last year I tried my hand at hockey. It was fun, but I wasn't particularly good at it. A few minutes later, I hear whimpering and barking from the lake. I

look out and see that there is a dog about 20 feet from the shore stuck on the ice.

I cannot leave a dog stranded. So, I quickly find a pathway down to the water and stop long enough to strap on the traction straps to my shoes. Slowly, I make my way out to the dog. Even though I saw others playing on the ice, I don't want to take any chances. No one even knows I'm out here.

After a few minutes, I make it to where the dog was slipping on wet ice. I put my hand down to let him sniff. Once the dog trusts me, I gently lift it and place it down a few steps away. Immediately, the dog gets traction and runs to the shore and doesn't stop.

I do a little happy dance. It feels good to be the hero even if that dog doesn't care and no one knows. I start my trek back to the shore when my foot slips and dips into the freezing water. The ice has broken under my foot and I can hear more cracking. I try to free my leg as the ice under my other foot tips and I fall. Falling into the pain and heat. Logically, I know the water is actually ice cold, but it feels like fire as I'm falling under. Trying to find up, I open my eyes to insane pain, but I see light. I reach for the light, kicking and paddling hard to get to it. I touch the light and…

CHAPTER TWO

FROM THE DEPTHS

I touch the light, and all the pain leaves my body. I am still underwater and cannot breathe, but that does not concern me. Streaking past me, I notice what looks like an arrow with a thin rope tied to it. I'm still trying to decide if I should grab it when my hand, of its own free will, latches on. Then the other, and soon they are working to pull me along the rope.

After what seems like a lifetime, powerful hands are grabbing at me and pulling me from the freezing water. My head is spinning and I'm in a daze, but I still feel no pain. I'm being carried out of the water.

With great effort, I force my eyes open and look up at my savior's face. I see perfect, smooth features and long platinum hair that barely cover what appear to be pointy ears. That strikes me as odd, but who am I to judge my hero's cosplay outfit in my time of need?

The one carrying me, the elf, says, "Where should we leave this young one?"

Another voice from an unknown companion says, "Olon, you fool, the boy will die if we don't help him. And you are not much better. We must warm you both."

Olon says, "Duri, you amaze me. Even an unmitigated fool can be correct in the proper situation. Please run ahead and start a great fire to melt away this biting cold."

My eyes close of their own will.

Slowly, I awaken in a cozy wrap of blankets that are so nice and warm I do not want to move, but my mind is screaming to me I'm in danger. I open my eyes, staring directly into a glorious fire and clearly the source of most of my warmth. I pull off the blankets and realized I'm not wearing anything. A few feet away, I see my clothes stacked near the fire. I reach out to them and find they are dry and warm. Odd, as I was expecting them to still be wet.

I fumble under the blankets to get dressed. Even with this fire, I don't want to expose my naked skin to the winter air. After the gymnastics of getting dressed, I sit cross-legged in front of the fire and inspect my surroundings. It's early morning, from the look probably around 7 AM. It's an overcast but bright morning and I'm sitting in the clearing at the seasonal campsite off the lake a few miles south of where Heidi's dad lives. I've spent a few weeks in the summer here for many years.

After a few minutes, two figures approach. One is tall with platinum hair and pointed ears. This must be my savior, Olon. The other is shorter and looks like, well, a dwarf from LOTR with shoulders as broad as his smile and lots of dark hair. This one must be Duri.

I wait to speak until they get within earshot. "Thank you for pulling me from the water. I owe you my life. I don't mean to sound ungrateful, but why are an elf and dwarf in Ironhaven?"

Olon makes a grunt of surprise.

Duri, however, breaks out in a laughter and says, "I told you this kid was special."

Olon says, "Boy, how are you able to see us? Let me clarify. How are you able to determine we are elf and dwarf?"

I take several moments to stop laughing. Duri's laughter doesn't help. "Well, there are the ears, hair, and eyes you sport. That and Duri, he just fits the part of dwarf perfectly."

Duri comes and sits next to me. Patting my back as his butt hits the ground. "I like this one."

Olon stands on the other side of the fire just staring at me. "What magic have you? It takes magic to see through the spell of hiding we have up. I suspect magic also kept some of the cold at bay for you."

"Magic? I know a dumb card trick, but other than that, I don't have a magic bone in me."

Olon tilts his head and studies me. His gaze feels like it's burning through to my very soul.

Olon walks around the fire to sit by Duri. "I see that is the truth, at least as you know it. But there is definitely something magic about you. However, I cannot surmise what. I do not sense any animosity inside you. As for pulling you out of the water, you are welcome. It was your choice to save the dog that convinced me you were worth saving."

Duri hands me a flask. "Drink. Even with the water you swallowed, you need more. What shall we call you, lad?"

I accept the flask and take a few drinks. "My

name is Tannin." Duri hands me a few bars of an incredibly tasty granola like substance and I eat it in silence. As I'm eating Duri packs up all the blankets and the lean to I didn't even notice that cover it. All of it he puts into an especially small bag that does not seem to grow as he loads it. Clearly some sort of magic bag. I watch him, mesmerized by the apparent magical feat of a bag that must be bigger on the inside.

Olon breaks the silence. "Tannin of Ironhaven, it is a good name. So Tannin, what had you walking down that path where you spotted the dog on the lake so late at night?"

With that prompting, I remember being dumped. It doesn't hurt as badly, but it still sucks. "I was supposed to pickup my now ex-girlfriend for a date a mile or so north of there. She dumped me and I was not in the right headspace to drive. So I thought it best to take a walk and calm down. But I never intended to swim."

Olon laughs in a melodious tone that brings a smile to my lips. He says, "Sorry for your loss in love, Tannin, but you did not need to drown your sorrows."

Something behind me falls, and I hear Duri fake shock. He says, "Do my ears deceive me? Did I hear

the uppity elf make a joke? And a fine one at that. Are you turning into a bard on me?"

Olon says, "Duri, you beg me to sing, you beg me to play, you beg me to brighten your day. And now you call me a bard. Ungrateful earth worm."

This exchange makes me think these two have been friends for longer than I can imagine.

"I am in both of your debt. Is there anything I can help you with?"

CHAPTER THREE
A WORTHY QUEST

Duri comes and joins us again by the fire. "Tannin, we are on a simple quest. However, this quest requires us to visit several locations each several days walk apart. Time is of the essence, and we lack any form of travel faster than walking. You mention driving. May I inquire what you drive?"

"I drive a modest car, one left to me from my grandfather. Nothing special, but it runs after it warms up."

Olon takes interest. "Your car. Can it fit the three of us?"

"It can absolutely fit us all. Can I offer to drive you somewhere?"

Olon says, "Our quest is simple and should be reasonably safe. We have five locations where we must place enchantments that will boost a spell to help locate a missing item. If you could drive us, that would be of great help and more that cover any perceived debt you believe you owe."

"I'd be happy to. It's Saturday and I have this weekend off from work. We need to walk about two miles to get to my ride."

Duri gets up and offers a hand to help me stand. "Welcome to our small party and our simple location quest, Tannin. If the fire has fully thawed you, we should make way."

I grab my coat and we start the trek back to my car. We walk in companionable silence for most of the way when it occurs to me. "Earlier, you showed surprise that I could see your true forms. What did you think I would see?"

Olon looks at me sideways. "The spell should make us appear to be boys your age. I trust Ironhaven doesn't have more magic users, so we should present that way for anyone else we run into."

We get to my car and I start it up. Olon gets in

the front passenger seat and Duri sits in the back. "It will take about ten minutes to warm up. So where is it you want me to take you?"

Duri pulls out a map and hands it to Olon. It's an exquisite hand-drawn map with absolutely no roads on it. Olon points out five markers on the map. "We need to go to these five locations in no particular order."

I laugh. "OK, I hope my phone works because I need to see the roads to navigate there."

This was the first I thought about my phone, and in my core I hope it will work. I haven't seen a road map since I was 6 and used it as wrapping paper for grandpa. As I reach for my pocket, I feel a tingling on my finger, like almost a static shock. As I pull my phone out, I notice I have a silver-white band on my ring finger of my right hand. I've never had a ring, but it just feels right and I don't even mention it.

"What was that?" Olon says, looking around as if someone was about to attack us.

"I just pulled out my phone and I hope after the little swim I had, it still works." I turn it on with no problem. It dings a few times and I have two messages from my mom and one from Heidi. I ignore the one from Heidi and read my moms. She ended up having to work all night, then apologizes

that she missed me this morning before I left. I texted back, I'm hanging out with friends and I love her. Luck was on my side and I won't get in trouble for being out all night.

I pull up my maps, and using the hand-drawn map, I pin five locations. The hand-drawn map was incredibly accurate for land features, making locating them fairly simple. "I've mapped the places you want to go. Three of them seem to be right off roadways. Two of them may be a bit of a hike from the road."

Duri asks, "Will that be a problem?"

"It shouldn't be." I study the locations, and the nearest one is a place I know well. I let out a quick laugh. "The closest is where I work a few nights a week. It's almost lunchtime and would be a great place to start and to get a warm meal."

Duri says, "Your call on the order but I could absolutely go for a warm meal."

We start the drive to Jerry's Good Eats. It's about a 15 minute drive because of construction. Duri is enjoying the drive. Olon, however, looks to be a few shades lighter.

"Olon, don't watch the trees go by. Only look forward or concentrate on something stationary in the car. It seems you may get motion sickness in a car. I recognized it because my cousin does the same thing."

Olon looks down and after a minute says, "Thank you, that helps. I can ride horses, boats and flying beasts without issue. Strange that this affects me."

We pull up to Jerry's and I park the car. "The map marks the actual building itself. Do you need to do your thing inside?"

Olon, looking much better, says, "No, the roof should suffice."

"Good, let's get out and I'll buy us all lunch. We can sit for a few until some of the crowd dies down. It typically does in about 45 minutes."

We choose outdoor seating. This time of year Jerry has heaters out to take a little off the chill. I translate the menu for both of them and get some ideas about what they would like. Difficult since they are not familiar with most of the menu items, so I mostly pick for them. I go order a few burgers, fries and three milkshakes. Jerry himself was there, and he hooked me up with some larger than normal sizes for "growing boys." Several minutes later and he brings it to the table himself. Jerry is one of the main backbones of this community and is a great boss.

We eat and Duri and Olon are both pleased and surprised at how good this greasy food is. And the

milkshakes, those bring huge smiles to them both. Throughout the meal, we just discuss random things. They ask a lot about my life and they evade a bunch of questions about theirs.

After about forty minutes, the lunch crowd clears out and we talk about how they will get to the roof. They are getting up to leave when Layla slowly walks up.

I look at Olon and Duri, wink and say, "The restroom is back around the right side there."

They both take the hint.

Layla says, "Hi Tannin, may I sit with you while I wait for my dad?"

"Of course, Layla, you are always welcome at my table."

CHAPTER FOUR

WARM AND SWEET

Layla sits across from me and gives me the warmest smile. She is the kindest person with the most amazing smile I have ever seen. She smiles despite having leukemia that she has been fighting for years. Layla insists on working once a week, more to get out of the house and forget she is sick for a short while. Jerry has found work she can do sitting in his warm office. She tires easily and the walk from the office to the bench was likely enough for her to need to rest.

Layla cinches up her coat. "Thank you. My dad

should be here in a few minutes to pick me up. Who are your friends? I don't believe I've seen them before."

I hate the idea of lying to Layla, but the circumstance requires it. "Olon is the taller one, and the other is Duri. They are distant cousins on my mom's side. They seem cool, but won't be here long."

She accepts that without question. Good, because I don't want to dig a hole of lies that I will just fall into later.

She gives me a serious look. "You can ask. I don't mind."

When Layla first got sick, I quickly saw how everyone always asks how she's feeling or how the sickness is going. Everyone wants details on every aspect of her sickness, often overlooking the girl in front of them. I decided right then that I would be the one person who treats Layla as a girl and not a sick girl.

"Are you getting excited about Christmas? The party is what, two weeks away?"

Layla graces me with the sweetest smile, and her eyes glaze over ever so slightly. She reaches across the table and holds both my hands. Her hands getting lost in the size of mine. "Thank you."

She lets that linger for a minute before continuing. "I am excited. I love this time of year with the snow and the lights. The party is the high-point and I cannot wait. You are coming? Right?"

"I wouldn't miss it. A chance to share great food and great hot chocolate with the best person I know."

Shyly, she asks, "Will you be bringing Heidi?"

This is the first time I've thought of Heidi today. Am I over her this soon? Maybe that shows we truly were over.

"No. Heidi broke up with me."

Layla gives my hands a good squeeze. "I'm sorry Tannin. She made a huge mistake that I'm sure she will regret."

Whenever I talk with Layla, it's clear why everyone loves this girl. Nearly the whole town, at least those that matter, would do anything for this girl. Most would trade places with her if it was possible. I know I would. I've made lots of material wishes through the years, as I'm sure everyone has. But the one genuine wish I have ever muttered is for the powers that be to cure Layla, and if required, put the sickness on me.

At that moment, the world changed, and I was looking at another level of definition. Everything and

everyone seemed muted except for Layla, who was in raging vivid color, and she looked stunning. A white haze, almost like a contained snow storm, emanated from my right hand. It snaked up and around Layla with tentacles reaching out to almost everyone in view. No one else seems to notice, at least to the best I can tell, with my eyes locked on Layla.

The vision lasts for what seems like three seconds and then instantly transitions back to the reality I know. It is jarring, but not in a bad way.

Layla shivers for a moment, then pulls her hands away to cinch up her coat more. "Brr, quite the chill out here today."

I don't have time to think about what just happened as Layla's dad pulls in. He gets out to walk over and help her, but I beat him to it. I gently help Layla to the passenger seat of her dad's car. Before she gets in, she gives me a hug. "Thank you Tannin."

"Thank you. And be sure to save a dance for me at the party."

I close the door, and Layla's dad is looking at me. He pats me on the shoulder and says, "You're a good person Tannin, never lose that."

I watch the car for a moment before I notice that Olon and Duri are at my side.

Olon looks a little alarmed. "Can we please head

to the car? I have questions I need answers to and I do not wish to be overheard."

I agree, and we get in my car and I start it up. "OK, what's up?"

Olon grabs my hand and inspects the ring. "Take this off."

I try to, but it won't budge or even turn. "I cannot. It's like it's a part of me."

Olon tries to turn it with no luck. "When did you get this ring?"

"I woke up this morning with it. But it seems like I have had it forever. I wasn't concerned, and honestly, I'm still not concerned."

Olon makes a harrumph sound.

Duri asks, "Did the people at the restaurant dislike or hate your friend?"

"Layla? No, everyone loves Layla."

Duri says, "She looks ill. Do people resent that?"

"No, Layla has leukemia and almost everyone she knows would give their life for her. I would. I know why you're asking, but I have no answers. That was the weirdest thing."

Olon's piercing eyes fixate on me. "Describe what you experienced."

I describe it in great detail. Both Olon and Duri ask several clarifying questions.

Olon says, "In real-time what you described happened in less than a half second. None of the other humans would have noticed it. I saw it because it was magic, but what I saw had a darker look and was only in real-time. Based on your descriptions, I suspect it was not an attack, but some sort of beneficial magic. Let me see your hand again."

Olon grabs my hand and says a few words I can not understand that have the feel of power to them. On the ring, engravings highlight and Olon quickly studies them. "Interesting! This ring identifies itself as the Ice Ring of Will. I've heard stories about this ring, but everyone presumed them to be fables. Some call it a wish ring, and others a ring of death and destruction. I suspect its nature is based on the bearer. No one knows how it works or how to find it. It's said that all who have wielded it can not recall doing so."

CHAPTER FIVE

A QUESTING WE WILL GO

We were quiet for a few minutes. Finally, I had to ask. "So, what does that mean?"

Olon drew a large breath before speaking. "I don't know. I don't sense any malice in you, and your actions have been nothing but honorable. It's uncertain what just happened, but I'm inclined to believe it was something good. There is nothing we can do about the ring and we probably shouldn't even try. You have become infinitely more interesting in some ways, but utterly boring in others."

Duri laughs. "So we are exactly where we were this morning, a strange magical companion on a just quest."

Olon says, "Again Duri, you surprise me with your astute observations of our situation without actually telling us anything."

To that Duri smiles, like he bested Olon in a match of strength. "Alright young Tannin, let's get to questing."

Getting the car back on the road, I turn on my favorite alt rock station and enjoy the attempts at singing and car dancing that Duri entertains us with while driving out to the second location. "I'm taking us to the sites we need to do a little hiking to get to first. I'm hoping we can get those done before the day gets away from us."

Olon says, "Good idea. Though Duri and I do well in lower light situations, it would be good to avoid the bitter cold that comes with it."

It takes about 15 minutes to arrive at a gravel road that will get us a little closer. Several minutes down this road, I spot a widened area. Likely an area used to park for hunting. It's that wooded out here that I'm sure at least bow hunters frequent it. "This is as close as I can drive. Your mark looks to be a quarter mile from here."

The direction I point is dense without great pathways.

Olon says, "I shall proceed alone for this one. I can move faster through this rough terrain than either of you."

Duri kicks his feet up on to the other side of the back seat and lays down. "You sure you won't be afraid of being alone in those deep dark woods, sir prissy wood elf?"

Olon doesn't even honor that with a response and is gone into the woods in a blink of an eye. I try to search for him with no luck.

Duri says, "Give up trying to follow his moves. He's at home in the woods and is likely almost to the location already. The only problem he will run into is stopping to smell a rotten log or mushroom."

"So what led to you and Olon traveling together? It's obvious you have been friends for a long time."

Duri sits up. "Truth of it be, I cannot remember it clearly. Some mates of mine took me to a pub near our encampment. We were traveling back home after selling some wares in a distant city. Someone bet something and I ended up in a drinking contest. Of course I won, but somewhere along the way a group of elves took it upon themselves to outdo us. No way in the depths they could, but try they did, and

good ole Olon was their glorious champion. Then, urged by all bystanders, we tried to out-drink each other. I'm told I won by three seconds. The next day, I awoke in a pile of hay with the fool curled up in my lap. It was dwarven ale we drank, none of that prissy elf piss they prefer. Gives an elf a hell of a hangover."

"OK, that's how you met. How did you become friends?"

Duri looks me dead in the eye and says, "Ah, well, that's where it gets interesting. See, his friends came to find him and my friends came to find me and, well, a fight ensued. A good ole fist fight and I think everyone on both sides was smiling. Them bitching about the ale, us bitching about them being bitchy. It was a grand ole time. But the local authority didn't think so. The barn got destroyed. The bar was repairable, but just barely. Several carts got damaged and the pile of us could only laugh about it. The mayor of the small town demanded we all stay and fix everything we broke. It took three weeks, but we honored the request. And in those three weeks, I laughed so much that Olon and I bonded over it. We have often traveled together since."

I share a laugh with Duri as Olon climbs back

into the car. That really didn't take him long. He must be fast.

Olon says, "I heard you were telling the story of us meeting Duri. Just know it was I that won by three seconds."

For the next twenty minutes and the full drive to the next location, they were good-nature bickering. It was like watching the old married couple in the townhome next to my father's place.

The next location was up Ironhaven hill on the other side of town. Again we drive up a gravel road, but this time I park in a parking area beside a fence that blocks the rest of the way up the hill we have come to.

CHAPTER SIX

SATURDAY DRIVE ABOUT TOWN

The fence is high and has barbed wire, but that stopped nothing but cars. The fence is the width of the road, with thick poles on each side that go down deep into the steep slopes. But every teen in Ironhaven knows that you just hold on to the pole and swing around. There is even a cement ledge to place your feet. I'm sure every mother would have a fit over seeing a kid go around this, but not a single kid of the thousands has ever fallen.

After swinging past, Duri turns and looks at the

gate. "It's not great for security, so what's the purpose?"

"The sole purpose of that gate is to keep older teens from driving up here on a weekend to have a party."

Olon gives me a sly look. "And does that stop them?"

"No, not in the least. It's just makes the walk longer."

We share a few jokes and I share with them the few stories I have from my times up here.

We walk up the incline. The gravel road snakes around the hill and leads to a fire lookout station. We hike about halfway up and then turn off into a thickly wooded darker area. Following a well-worn path, we hike only about 100 yards in until we find a large clearing. Olon asks Duri and me to wait here while he continues a few feet further and does his magic thing.

Duri asks, "This is the party spot, isn't it? I can see the remnants of lots of people and enormous bonfires."

"I honestly cannot tell you, but you are probably correct. Each time I came up here, I was not leading. If this is not the spot, there are others very similar."

Duri teases me a bit before Olon finds his way

back and we make our way back to the car. The hike back was nicer, as it was downhill most of the way. As we are getting to the main gravel road, the sun disappears below the other side of the hill. It gets dark pretty fast on this side, so I pull out my cell phone and turn on the flashlight feature, which provides more than enough light to keep us on the gravel track and make our way back to the car.

Once in the car, I pull up the navigation app on my phone. "The next three locations are pretty easy to get to. We can drive up pretty close to each."

Duri says, "Are any near an eatery? I could certainly go for another delightful meal."

"Yeah, the second one is near a pizza place that is pretty good. However, I'm running short on cash and don't get paid for a few days. I'm afraid I cannot afford to buy us dinner."

Olon seems surprised. "I'm sorry. I should have thought of that. Of course, someone of your age would not have a great deal of money. We should not have taken advantage of your kindness. Do you have any of your paper money now? I think I can help."

Without even thinking twice about it, I hand over my emergency twenty.

Olon scrutinizes it, surveying every portion, then

chants a complex set of words that I cannot make out. Suddenly, there is a small pile of money forming between us on the front seat. "Is this enough?" He asks, as a pile of about twenty appear.

"Way more than enough, but what did you do? If you duplicated it, any machine will catch the duplicate numbers." I say with a slight panic in my voice.

Olon laughs for a moment, "Tannin, that is a mistake I made when much younger on my first quest. No, duplicating them would probably get you in trouble. What I did was summon lost money of the same denomination. These bills are from miles around and are only lost bills that no one would ever find. There is so much money in your world that is just lost that this is effective and fairly risk free."

"Wow, I would never have thought of that. It's hard to believe someone could lose a twenty."

Olon hands me the original twenty-dollar bill, and I put it back in my special emergency section of my wallet. I count up the rest and it's around $500. I try to hand it to Olon, and he refuses telling me to use it for dinner and lodging for the night.

We get to the third stop and it's at an industrial complex that is still under construction. I'm able to get within twenty feet of where Olon needs to go.

He gets out to do this one himself and asks us to wait.

"This quest seems pretty easy." I say, not really to anyone.

Duri laughs and says, "They all start out like this. Let's just hope saving you was the most action we see."

I had already forgotten about last night. Strange how keeping busy can keep your mind off things.

"Yeah, that was eventful enough for me, too."

Within five minutes, Olon is back, and I head towards Pappa Pete's Pizza on the outskirts of town. In my opinion, the thin crust pizza with the cup and char pepperoni makes it the best pizza anywhere.

We pull up to Pappa Pete's parking lot and Olon asks us to give him several minutes to perform his magic. Duri and I sit quietly, both drooling from the smell of pizza baking, as we wait for him. It takes longer than expected, but after about fifteen minutes, Olon is back in front of the car. He apologizes as he had to wait for a lull in foot traffic to climb up to the roof.

Then we head into Pappa Pete's for a glorious meal.

CHAPTER SEVEN

THERES A STORY

Pappa Petes isn't busy yet. It's on the pricier side for pizza and sometimes it gets less traffic. As we walk in, there is a sign that says seat yourself. We find a great seat, and I help Duri and Olon decipher the menu. Duri agrees my favorite sounds good and Olon is interested in a salad.

After a few minutes, a woman who looks like the typical grandmother comes over to take our order. I've seen her the few times I've been here with my dad. He told me her husband died, and financially she needs to work instead of enjoying retirement, but

she claims to any who asks that she works for the company of others. She takes our order and tells Olon to help himself to the salad bar when he is ready. When she walks away, I explain the salad bar to him.

We are chatting about the restaurant when the server comes back with our drinks. I notice she is favoring one leg and seems to struggle with the tray. My grandmother is like that. She has arthritis and sometimes it's painful in her joints. I don't know the server really at all, I only get the impression she is a really pleasant woman who has had some bad turns in life. I wish she didn't get those pains that are bothering her. That her joints wouldn't cause her to have difficulty doing her job and that her life was just a little easier.

I feel a tingling in my hand as the woman is putting down our pitcher of soda. Suddenly, my hand is glowing, but only Olon seems to notice. A white fog spreads from my hand to the older serving woman and washes over her, denser over her joints. It lasts for only a second and is gone.

The server stumbles just slightly as she is placing an empty glass in front of me. "I'm sorry. I don't know what came over me. Good thing that wasn't full of soda," she says with a warm smile.

She walks away and I notice she is no longer favoring one leg and is standing slightly straighter.

Olon asks, "What were you thinking about when she was serving us?"

"I was just thinking how unfair it was that she must work at her age and that her joints are bothering her. I wished I could make her life a little better by removing that pain."

Olon smiles, "I think maybe you have. Be careful what you wish for young Tannin of Ironhaven. This was a noble request, but even in the best of us, occasionally our minds can be petty. That ring has given you an amazing gift, but a gift is only as noble as its bearer. Check your thoughts. You must ensure you do not unintentionally hurt someone."

Olon and Duri ask me many questions about my life as we await our meal. When the pizza arrives, the questions shift to learn more about them both, but at a much slower pace. Duri and I are enjoying the pizza so much that Olon had to try it. It's no surprise that they are both fans of my favorite pizza now. Who wouldn't be?

Wiping my hands after having my last piece, I glance around the establishment and I see her. My ex, Heidi, is in a booth on the other side of the restaurant, staring at me with malice. My heart breaks

seeing she is with Jake, the quarterback of the football team. I'm not so much hurt we broke up as I'm sad she is with him. He has a reputation of dating a girl and dumping them. Even worse is he then spreads rumors about the girls. While he may be popular, I think he is disgusting and I'm sad that Heidi might find herself attracted to someone like him.

I turn back to Olon and Duri to ask them to leave when Heidi gets up and walks over to the table and says, "Why are you here? Are you so petty that you would ruin my date?"

Jake shuffles up beside her and puts his arm around her shoulders.

Heidi gives a crooked smile to Jake and then focuses back on me. "Well, why are you here?" Heidi says with attitude.

I only get out, "What? I have no clue…," before Heidi cuts me off.

She says, "You are only here to ruin my night."

I don't know where this is coming from, but I'm getting mad. More than mad, I'm saddened by how she is acting towards me just days after being so sweet and caring. I question how she treated me. Was she faithful? Was this relationship with Jake going on before we broke up? I slow down and see

how negative I'm getting, and notice a feeling of coldness emanating from my hand. I focus on it and see a dark fog forming.

Olon notices too and gets up to stand between Heidi and I. "Miss, I don't know you or your friend, but I think you are mistaken. My cousin and brother decided on this restaurant randomly and any intent you are inferring from our presence is purely on your part. I must also point out that we have been here much longer than you and your friend and we are, in fact, getting ready to leave. So please don't cause a scene."

Oh crap, that totally hits me sideways. The dark fog disappears and I laugh.

Heidi looks pissed, and Jake seems bored.

"You broke up with me and I accept that. I wish only the best for you. However, I will never, ever stalk you. This is a small town and you will see me occasionally. Do yourself a favor and accept that. I will not hide so that you don't have to face your personal guilt. It's over between us. Please act that way."

I grab my coat and stand up to go. Jake is standing in the way, but moves back and gives me a smile and a fist bump. That appears to bother Heidi, but she is so shaken by what I said that she says no

more. Duri and Olon follow my lead. We stop by the counter to pay, tipping the server well, then head out to the car.

Once in the car, Duri says, "So that was your former girlfriend? With your disposition, I figured you would have picked a nicer person."

"Until two nights ago, she was nicer. She broke up with me with no warning and I had no clue it was coming. But that personality in there is nothing I've ever seen."

Olon sighs. "Breakups can change people, and your remarks were on target. She likely convinced herself that she would never see you after she dumped you. And seeing you now likely brings up some guilty feelings. It's the way of the world, both hidden and visible. She should have handled it better. You, however, did better than I expected. There was definitely something dark trying to take hold. Your hand looked like coal for a moment and I feared something bad. But you held it back. Good job."

"I felt it and what you did helped. It scared me and I thought something bad could happen too. Thank you."

I sat there for a few minutes while the car warmed up, just gathering my thoughts. I was OK that Heidi and I were not together anymore. Out of

the blue, Duri farts, and it was so bad we had to evacuate the car. My god, dwarf farts suck. Olon won't stop teasing Duri about it as we drive to the last location.

CHAPTER EIGHT

AND THE PLAN IS

We arrive at the last location, which is at a supermarket. Olon and Duri both ask me to stay in the car while they place the last enchantment which will go somewhere on top of the store. While waiting, I check my phone and see I have a text from my mom apologizing for not seeing me yesterday or today. She also lets me know she has to work the night shift again. She says, since we won't see each other, I can go to my dad's a day early if I want. I send back a message she probably will not get for hours when she has her lunch break. In my message,

I tell her I'm not sure which house I will stay at, but I'll be safe either way and I'll call her in a few days on her next day off.

I'm scrolling through some dumb social media posts when I get another message. It is from Heidi. It starts off OK as she asks for forgiveness for what she said to me at Papa Pete's. But an instant after that message arrived, I got another one with her asking me to not be so jealous of her and Jake. Wow, I really wanted to reply that I was only sad, but I knew that wouldn't get taken well, so I ignore the texts. We are no longer dating, so she cannot expect I'll always reply right away. I need to set up my boundaries, and this is only one of them.

The moment I put my phone down, it dings with another message. I take a deep steadying breath because I figure it is her again. I am so very glad I was wrong. When I see the name, I can't help but smile.

Layla: *Hey Tannin, for some bizarre reason I'm still awake and I just wanted to say hi and let you know that I really appreciate you*

If you need someone to talk to, I'm here

Me: *Thanks. I think I'm OK, but thank you for the offer*

Layla: *Anytime*

  I heard a rumor about a run in at a pizza place

Me: *Yeah, nothing big. She thought I was following her or something*

  I'm not!

  I'm over her and that's not me

Layla: *I didn't think for a minute it would be*

I see that Olon and Duri are walking back to the car.

Me: *Hey Layla, I'm driving now and cannot talk*

  Sorry

Layla: *OK, be safe!*

  Hey the way I'm feeling, I will be up for hours

  If you want to, message me when you are home

Duri says, "That's an awfully stupid grin. You hitting on a girl or something?"

Olon looks at me, then laughs and laughs some more.

"Yeah, I was messaging my mom."

Duri slumps down in the back seat. "Oh, I'm

sorry. I was not very sensitive about that. Like hell, that's not the look of someone talking to their mom."

Changing the subject, I say, "So where to next?"

Olon gains his composure then says, "Now we must wait twelve hours. Then I will do a locater spell using the enchantments to amplify it. Thanks to you, we are days ahead of where we would be. Would you be so kind as to help us find lodging?"

I think for a minute. "How old do you appear to others?"

Olon says, "Your age or slightly older."

"OK, so there are two places. One is kinda sketchy and lets anyone with cash rent regardless of age. The beds suck and it's dirty. The other is nicer but makes the rooms available to 17 and older. Which do you prefer? The money you gave me should cover either for a night or two."

Duri says, "I hate to say it, but the sketchy one we would be less likely to be noticed. But before we go, can we go shopping for some things?"

"Of course, and we are at a store if your things are food and drinks."

Duri says, "Yes, perfect. Can we also get ale here?"

"While they sell it, you are not old enough to buy

it and don't have the proper ID."

Olon says, "Don't worry Duri, I'll get the ale."

I don't even want to know. We do a little shopping and the Dwarf really likes his junk food.

After that, I drive them a few blocks away to the sketchier of the motels. I hand the money to Olon and he heads to the office to get a room after a little coaching from me. I don't want to do it as the guy working knows my dad and he would tell him I rented a room.

It takes almost twenty minutes before Olon comes back with a key. He has a little map of the motel and has me drive to the back, where their room is on the ground floor. I help them take the food bags into the room.

"So, would you like me to come back tomorrow to help you?"

Olon says, "You have helped us a tremendous amount already. I would not want to put you out."

"Nonsense. It gets me out of the house. I don't work tomorrow and this will give me something to do. I could be here at noon."

Duri says, "That would be great and we would appreciate the help."

Olon looks at Duri for a minute, then turns to me. "Yes, thank you. We would love the help.

Tomorrow I will cast the spell and we can track down the amulet."

I bid my farewells and decide to stay at my mom's place. The drive to her house is uneventful. After a quick snack, I decide to see if Layla is still up for chatting. She is, and I end up staying up much later than expected, having a pleasant conversation with her. I miss being able to talk to Layla for hours on end, and this is nice.

CHAPTER NINE

THE BIG BAD

I woke up much later than normal and I take some time to get moving. It's getting near noon so I get ready to go. I do it quietly so as not to wake my mom. She works hard and needs all the sleep she can manage. Before I head out, I leave a note for her telling her I have some errands today and will stay at Dad's house tonight. Grabbing my bag containing what possessions I ferry between the two houses, I head out to warm up my car.

I get in my car, after scraping the windows and brushing off the light dusting of snow we got

overnight, hoping it has warmed up enough to circulate warm air. Of course it hasn't, so I shiver while checking for any new messages on my phone. There was just one I haven't seen from Layla telling me to have a great night. That is sweet, and I am sorry I missed it before I crashed last night.

A few minutes later, I arrive at the sketchy hotel where Olon and Duri have a room. I knock and Duri lets me in. The room smells of Popeyes Chicken and there are two large baskets of it sitting on the small table. Duri tells me to help myself and my grumbling stomach agrees. I grab a piece and scarf it down.

After using toilet paper to wipe my hands, I ask, "So, where is Olon?"

Duri says, "He should be back soon. I'm not sure he really needs to, but he feels more comfortable performing many spells in the woods. So he's somewhere back behind us, doing his magic thing."

We chat about random things while each of us eats a bit more. OK, not random. Duri grills me about what I hope to find when I'm checking my phone every two minutes. I tell him I'm expecting a message from my mom, but he's not buying it.

He is laughing at my blushing when Olon comes back into the room. Olon looks tired, like he played

video games all night long tired. He sits on the bed and Duri hands him a bucket of chicken. Olon tears into it like I've only seen the football players do after a long practice. A few minutes of eating seems to bring back his energy.

"Thank you for helping us again today, Tannin of Ironhaven. I have located the Amulet of Irini we seek," he says as he shows me a point on his map.

Pulling out my phone, I first check my messages, then pull up the map app. I find the spot his map identified. "Looks like that is in the field, or perhaps the woods behind Ironhaven high school. Good thing the school is closed for winter break. It should be pretty empty."

Olon says, "That is good. I must warn you, I know the amulet is there, but I do not know what or who is with the amulet. We suspect it is with someone or something, but I cannot see what that is. There could be an individual or a group."

Duri says, "That said, we must approach this area with caution. We need to get a view of what is going on before we charge in and kick butt."

I grab the notepad the hotel has on the desk and draw a little map of the high school. "You identified this area in the back behind the baseball fields. There are woods along here and between the woods and

the baseball fields is open grass. If we park up front and go around the far end of the school, we can travel along the woods and not get noticed as we approach."

Duri smiles at me and gives my shoulder a nudge.

Olon says, "Great plan Tannin, the woods should provide ample cover and I can help us blend in a little."

After a few more minutes of chatting about the area, we drive to the high school. On the way, I have to stop for gas and, of course, Duri wants some snacks from the station's convenience store.

I park in front of the school on the street as the gates to the parking area are closed. I lead them around the right side of the school and towards the woods that surround the school property.

Olon stops us once we arrive at the tree line. "Stay behind me. I will muffle any noises we make and help us blend into the tree line." He then mutters some words I cannot make out, but they have a powerful feel to them. Around us, I see something that looks like a shimmer of light in a loose bubble. Kind of like the heat haze you can see when on a sweltering summer day.

We follow Olon, as he slowly leads us along the

trees toward the baseball fields. He stops roughly every ten feet and scans the area intently. Occasionally murmuring things I cannot hear correctly or understand, but I assume are some type of magic.

After about ten minutes of slow moves, I spot something spectacular. Something that is so incredibly cute I want to play with it. "Is that a puppy? A 20 foot tall golden retriever puppy dog?"

We all stop, and no one says anything for several minutes until Duri breaks the silence. "By Moridans hammer, that is the biggest pup I've ever seen."

Olon turns to us, and his level of surprise is clear. "In all my days, I have never encountered a being of this nature. I have no information about this giant puppy, other than it looks fluffy and cute. If you look closely, you can see the amulet around its neck as if were a tag on a dog collar. I do not know what to expect when we approach this beast, but Tannin I must warn, you must not summon the power of the ring for any negative purposes like an attack. Please hang back and let Duri and I deal with the beast."

I begrudgingly agree to hang back. There is nothing more I would rather do at this moment than go play with that monster size golden retriever puppy. It seems to almost draw me in and I know it

would just love to play. I shake my head to clear it and the desire to run towards the puppy relaxes a little. I'm now worried the puppy has some spell or charm to lure people in.

Olon and Duri slowly approach the pup, Olon almost sliding around the side of the neck while Duri approaches it, holding his hand out palm up for the pup to sniff. The dog tentatively inspects Duri, then suddenly licks him, the tongue as large as Duri himself. Duri falls under a blanket of saliva, then the pup nudges him with its wet nose. Duri is laughing and appearing to have fun.

Olon has made his way to the chain holding the amulet to the pup's neck and slowly draws his knife to sever the chain.

Before Olon could finish his move, a deep voice yells "Fluffy, defend!"

Then things get crazy.

CHAPTER TEN

WHEN PUPS ATTACK

In a blink of an eye, the world changes. The puppy swats Duri away and starts growling. However, it seems not to notice Olon.

Olon moves to take on the man who commanded Fluffy. This man is walking towards Olon from the woods. As he gets a little closer, I can see he looks to be an elf too, but seems to have a paler complexion and a larger build, although that is hard to be certain of under the full set of armor he wears. He draws a long sword to confront Olon and taunts him.

I turn my attention back to Duri, and he has a battle axe out defending blows from Fluffy, but is quickly being over powered. It looks like a dog playing with a toy.

I hear the clash of blades, a distinct sound I've never heard before but can easily identify with no thought. I'm not sure if my reaction to the sound is instinctive, protective, or just plain fear, but I don't like the sound of a sword fight.

Things are going super fast, nothing at all like the fights I have read about in books or watched in movies. It's not a drawn out battle where everyone is fighting for hours. It's fast and brutal.

Fluffy makes its move and I'm on my feet running before it finishes it. Fluffy locks his teeth around Duri's midsection and picks him up, swinging its head like it is attacking a chew toy. Then it releasing Duri in mid-shake and he goes flying into the backstop of the baseball field. He bounces off and hits the ground hard.

I'm running to assist, and I just hope Fluffy doesn't notice me. I feel a tingle on my right hand, and Fluffy looks the other way.

I get to Duri, and he looks to be in terrible shape. I try to find all the spots he's bleeding from and it's too many to count.

In a low and raspy voice, Duri says, "Tell me, boy, how does Olon fare?"

I relay to Duri that the sword chatter has lessened, and I can see them dancing around each other, tentatively looking for openings on their opponents. Olon looks to be bleeding from a cut on his side and a cut to his left arm. Right then, the other elf attacks with greater vigor and determined blows. Olon blocks the attacks, but you can see his energy failing. It's at this moment I know with absolute certainty he will fall.

Duri coughs up blood and I know he may not make it, as his injuries seem dangerously bad. I look from Duri to Olon and I don't know what I can do. I certainly cannot take on the warrior elf and help Olon. That would get me killed a second before Olon dies. I cannot do anything about Duri, as he doesn't even have time for me to drag him to the car.

With no other realistic options, I can only wish for a solution. I can wish that Duri is OK and has the skill and the power to help Olon defeat the other elf. I wish I can tame Fluffy to have it fight for me against the enemy elf, and wish that Olon is OK and all his wounds will instantly heal.

My hand burns with an intense fury, and a snowstorm develops around me. So thick it

envelopes the entire area surrounding me, Duri, Fluffy, and Olon. I find I am standing and, without thinking, I command, "Fluffy, to me!"

The puppy obeys and is instantly in front of me, bowing down as if it submits. My body is moving with purpose but without my conscious control. It instinctively leads me beside the puppy and I climb up on its back, grabbing the chain around its neck to control it.

Duri stands up and looks more confident than ever. He gives me a strange look, then runs to assist Olon. The apparent snowstorm that formed and is still raging momentarily distracts the warrior elf. Mentally, I order Fluffy to move in between the two elves, giving Duri and Olon a moment to strategize. The warrior elf recovers and tries to order Fluffy to obey his commands, but the puppy is only listening only to me. I order Fluffy to attack and the pup swats at the warrior elf with a front paw, knocking him back.

Olon and Duri use this chance to rush the warrior elf, but the warrior elf is very skilled and blocks both their attacks.

My control of the pup seems to be born of force of will and takes no verbal commands. I will the dog to get behind the warrior elf to block any retreat.

Olon and Duri work together in a whirlwind of motions that deflect any blow from the warrior elf and drive him back a few feet.

I use this opportunity to attack. I will Fluffy to swipe at the warrior elf's midsection and the paw connects. The blow tosses the elf down. Olon and Duri pivot to attack, and I will Fluffy to get behind the warrior elf again. Olon gives me a look of understanding and disengages a moment, using the time to tell Duri something. Duri gives me a nod and I hope they think what I'm thinking.

Olon and Duri attack again, but after a few swings, they move to the side away from each other and attack. This causes the warrior elf to keep looking between them and to back up a step. Duri and Olon press their attacks.

It's a great idea, and it gives Fluffy and me the time we need. As Duri and Olon attack, I will Fluffy to use its paw to push down on the upper section of the warrior elf's body to push him over face first. As the warrior elf falls, I will Fluffy to hold the elf down with its paw and all its weight.

Duri and Olon quickly move in and disarm the elf. Duri quickly hog ties the elf with a lead from arms to legs and neck. So with any quick pull of the rope, the elf's feet and arms will bind and choke him.

To my untrained eye, that seems very effective.

Duri and Olon tie the warrior elf to a tree, and I dismount. Olon walks up to Fluffy and takes the amulet, but leaves the chain. Duri ties a rope to the chain, and asks me to have the puppy sit.

The warrior elf lets out a stream of what I assume are curses. Olon says a few words that effectively silence the warrior.

Olon seems to make a fire out of nothing and we gather around. "Thank you Tannin of Ironhaven. Without your astute intervention, we would have certainly fallen today. I cannot state how important this amulet is to my people. And with the status of the other elf, you may have helped prevent a bloody war. Thank you."

Duri gives me a hug. "Today was to be my last day, as that dog was my downfall. Without your gifts, I know I would have taken my last breaths. And I thank you for a memory that I will spill over many drinks. The image of you riding that beast into battle. Bards will sing songs in your and Fluffy's honor."

CHAPTER ELEVEN

HAPPILY EVER AFTER

We warm up by the fire, and Olon and Duri tend to the few wounds they have. I healed most of their wounds with my magical intervention. The snowstorm dies down and, after about ten minutes, entirely stops.

I'm more tired than I can ever recall being. I know the walk back to my car will be a choir. It feels like the magic of the ring took more energy than the fight did.

Olon says, "Tannin, we must return to our realm with the amulet and our two prisoners immediately."

"Is Fluffy really a prisoner? The pup was only doing what the other elf commanded by magic."

Duri laughs. "So, you want to keep the beast, do you?"

"I would love to, but that is impossible and I could never afford to feed it. But really, can you let it go when you are in your realm or something?"

Olon gives me a long stare. "I will speak for the beast and ask the council to consider setting it free. You are a kind soul Tannin of Ironhaven. Please never change that."

"Where do you need to go to get back to your realm?"

"We can create a portal right here and return. We should get going, as there may be more work on our side that we must deal with. Duri, please gather the fluffy pup and I'll lead the warrior. Tannin of Ironhaven, I hope our paths cross again," Olon says as he shakes my hand.

Duri gives me a stern hug. "Tannin, gain a few years and we will share an ale reliving our conquest of warrior and beast. Live well and live loud. I too hope our paths cross again."

Olon steps to the side and chants something that creates a portal that they lead the warrior and Fluffy through.

I'm so tired, I think I'll sleep right here for a few minutes.

. . .

I wake up in an uncomfortable bed with no recollection of how I got here. The last thing I recall is seeing Olon and Duri walk through a portal with the warrior elf and Fluffy and wanting to sleep.

I find it's hard to open my eyes and there is pain over much of my body. I'm cold, but I can tell I have heated blankets covering me.

Ever so slowly, I pry my eyes open and find I'm in a hospital shivering. My father is asleep in a chair near me on the left and my mom is asleep with her head down on the bed and a chair scooted right next to it. I'm confused and have no clue what is going on.

A doctor walks in and sees I'm awake. "Tannin, you are in the hospital. You fell through ice on a lake while saving a dog. Several people who were playing on the ice nearby and saw you. By pure chance, they had a rope and one brave soul dove in to pull you out with it. You are very a lucky young man. You are not totally out of the woods, but things are progressing nicely and if we can get you warmed up, I expect your youthful body will bounce right back."

My mom and dad wake while the doctor is

talking to me. They have a million questions for the doctor and for me. I am confused, but that doesn't seem to bother anyone. I understand I can't start talking about elves, dwarfs, and super sized puppies. No one else can see their true forms and I'll sound crazy. I recall all the events, but it seems like the timeline got changed to where Olon didn't save me.

Over the next few days, I have doubts about my experience. I talk to a counselor, and they say it is common to have strange and vivid dreams with situations like this. Everything the doctors and my parents tell me makes it clear it is all in my head. I believe them, but there is some part of me that really wants the events to be true.

Some things happened like I recall them like Heidi hooking up way too quickly with Jake. Lots of questions about that, but I'll leave them be as it is not worth worrying about them. The counselor believes I must have seen the signs of the breakup coming and proposed that perhaps my subconscious put together the clues about them getting together. That feels like a convention explanation, but I don't have a better one.

After several days, I'm back from the hospital staying at my dad's house when I get a text from Layla to ask if I am alright. After assuring her I am

fine, she wants to make sure I am coming to the Christmas party. It would be great to see her and I could use some fun. I remember a conversation that I'm not sure really happened. I won't ask about it, but perhaps I can ask some of the same questions to find out if the conversation could have gone how I recall it.

Two days later is the party. I arrive before Layla and her family. After greeting several families I know, and ditching my mother with her close friends, I take a seat by the fire to enjoy the warmth. It may only be in my head, but I seem to feel cold easier than I used to.

I hear a commotion and notice people gathering at the hall entrance. Layla and her family enter to a flurry of people greeting them and asking questions. Layla is polite until she sees me, then she disengages and runs over and jumps in my lap. She looks amazing and is absolutely glowing.

Layla gives me a peck on the cheek and hugs me deeply. Then she leans her head back to look me in the eye. "Can you believe it? I'm healed." Seeing the confusion on my faces she says, "Oh, no one told you yet. Let me be the first to tell you I'm healed. The day after you fell in the lake, I started feeling fantastic and day after day I felt better. This made

my parents worry it was a sign of bad things, so they took me in for some tests. A few tests turned into lots of tests and that turns into I'm fine. Like I never had leukemia fine. Somehow I'm not just cured. It's like I never had leukemia at all."

All I could think of for a few minutes was about my wish and the ring. The ring I do not see on my finger, but I can feel the indentation left from it. "That is marvelous, Layla. I don't know what to say. It's a miracle for the only person I know that deserves a miracle."

I hear bustle and Layla and I both look up. Some old lady is holding mistletoe over our heads.

Layla looks at me with a smile. "I guess we must," and she kisses me. First it is tentative, but moves into a bit more passionate. Then brakes off. "I'm sorry, I just never."

"Don't be sorry for that. Ever."

After a few minutes of us staring into each other's eyes, I get the courage to say, "hey let's take a little walk around. Maybe we can find some more mistletoe."

Layla giggles. "No sir, right now I want you to take me to dance."

I notice a slow song is just starting. "Certainly, my dear. We shall dance the night away."

Call to Action

Please see https://miketconley.com, my author site, for
more information on my books.
While there, consider signing up for my entertainment
list:
https://miketconley.com/join-my-entertainment-list
This list will bet you access to monthly newsletters and
book release info.

As a special bonus, my monthly newsletters will include
links to free and discounted books by other authors or
myself.

Visit the website below and you can sign up to receive
emails whenever Mike Conley publishes a new book.
There's no charge and no obligation

https://books2read.com/r/B-A-KDKR-BXTUB

Thank you, Mike Conley

Other work by
Mike Conley

The After — Book 1 of the Afterverse

Destiny's Crow — Book 2 of the Afterverse (2023)

Past the Fall — serialized story on Kindle Vella (2022-2023)

Adam & Elese - An Afterverse Story — serialized story on Kindle Vella and will be on Kindle Unlimited and Amazon mid-2023

Social Links

Author site:
https://miketconley.com

Facebook Author page:
https://www.facebook.com/authormikeconley

TikTok:
https://www.tiktok.com/@miketconley_author

Instagram:
https://www.instagram.com/miketconley

YouTube Channel:
https://www.youtube.com/channel/UC3PEspi2DIy3Gfh8h-LMSQg

Author Mike Conley discord server:
https://discord.gg/22BBS3zC2B

About the Author

Mike T Conley is an author of Sci-Fi and Fantasy original fiction work. He is the Author of The After and other upcoming Afterverse novels.

Kylynn Conley is Mike's 11-year-old daughter.

Why would you, the reader, find me (Mike Conley) interesting? I'd like to say that I'm a charming master of all things. But that's just what I would like to say. The truth is somewhere south of that. I live and breath all things Sci-Fi and Fantasy. My day job is one that is immersed in software engineering leadership and technology that helps fuel a love for all types of technical things. I also have a passion for epic stories, often creating universes in my head and letting them run amuck. And yes, that costs me a lot of sleep. The idea of sharing my stories is so appealing, I started writing in my later-mid life.

As for why you would find my daughter amazing. She just is. Because of her age, I won't say much other than she is amazingly smart and fun.

www.ingramcontent.com/pod-product-compliance
Lightning Source LLC
Chambersburg PA
CBHW021341160726
47994CB00007B/2796